No Pooping on the Dock!

The Story About ---

| The Owl | The Looney Duck | The Whacky Duck | The Crazy Duck | The Naughty Duck |

Written and Illustrated by: Kristine Ochu
Inspired by: Fiona and Josephine Mingus
Copyright Protected 2017

Kristine Ochu
3-30-2018

It was a beautiful sunny morning at Grammy's lake. Fiona and Josephine were so happy to sit on the dock with Grammy and splash their feet in the water. Next to Grammy was their favorite owl statue that guarded the dock to scare the ducks away.

"Grammy, will you tell us the owl and duck story?" Fiona asked.

"Of course," Grammy said smiling at them. "One morning the owl was sitting on the dock, looking at the lake. He had blueberry pancakes for breakfast and was feeling so happy when suddenly a duck swam up."

"And the duck went---?" Grammy asked.

"Quack, quack," Josephine quacked.

"And the owl said---?"

"Who, who are you?" Fiona hooted.

"The duck said he was a looney duck and asked if he could sit on the dock. The owl said it was okay but there was no pooping on the dock. So the duck climbed on the dock, then guess what happened?"

"He pooped on the dock," Josephine chimed in.

"Yes!" Grammy replied.

"Oh no! Yucky, icky!" They all shouted as they made funny faces and shook their heads in dismay.

"The owl was so upset that he told the duck to leave right now and never come back! That night the owl went to bed hoping he would never see that looney duck again."

"The next morning, the owl got up and had his favorite crunchy cereal that made him smile. Afterwards he went outside to sit on the dock, then guess what happened?"

"The duck came back!" Fiona exclaimed.

"Yes, he did but now there were two ducks!"

"The two ducks swam up to the owl and said---?"

"Quack, Quack!" Josephine quacked.

"And the owl said---?"

"Who, who are you?" Fiona hooted.

"And it was---?

"A looney duck and a whacky duck," Fiona and Josephine said together.

"The ducks asked if they could come and sit on the dock. The owl said yes but there was no pooping on the dock. So the ducks hopped on the dock, then guess what happened?"

"They pooped on the dock!" Josephine shouted.

"Oh no! Yucky, icky!" They all groaned and moaned.

"The owl got so mad and yelled at them to leave right now. The ducks hopped off the dock and swam away. That night the owl had happy dreams because he believed that the looney and the whacky duck would never come back."

"The next morning the owl had scrambled eggs and bacon for breakfast and his tummy felt so good. He went out and sat on the dock and shook his head because he couldn't believe it! There were---?"

"Three ducks swimming to the dock!" Fiona exclaimed.

"And the ducks went---?"

"Quack, quack," Josephine quacked.

"And the owl went---?"

"Who, who are you?" Fiona hooted.

"That's right! And they were---?"

"A looney duck, a whacky duck and a crazy duck," Fiona and Josephine answered.

"You are so smart!" Grammy said as she gave them each a big hug.

"The owl warned them there was no pooping on the dock. So all three ducks waddled onto the dock, then guess what happened?"

"They pooped on the dock!" Fiona and Josephine shouted.

"Oh no! Yucky, icky!" They kicked their feet in the lake splashing water everywhere.

"This time the owl flapped his wings to scare the ducks and shooed them away. That night the owl went to bed and had bad dreams about the looney, whacky and crazy ducks."

"The next morning the owl had waffles and blueberries and felt all better. He went down to the dock and blinked his eyes. He couldn't believe it because now there were---?"

"Four ducks!" Fiona answered.

"And the ducks went---?"

"Quack, quack," Josephine quacked.

"And the owl went---?"

"Who, who are you?" Fiona hooted.

"And the ducks were---?"

"A looney duck, a whacky duck, a crazy duck and a naughty duck!" Fiona and Josephine replied.

"The owl said he would give them one more chance, but there was no pooping on the dock. So the four ducks scrambled up on the dock and they---?"

"Pooped! Yucky, icky!" They all giggled and rolled around the dock being silly.

"The owl got so mad that he jumped in the water. He flapped his wings and splashed water all over the ducks. Then the owl flew up in the air and chased those ducks far across the lake. The owl chased the ducks so far away that they never came back. Now the owl gets to sit here, look out on the lake and be happy."

"I love that story, Grammy," Fiona said.

"Me too," Josephine agreed.

"Should we go swimming now?" Grammy asked.

"Yes!" Fiona and Josephine exclaimed.

They all stood up and stretched. Grammy wiggled her way in between Fiona and Josephine so she could hold both of their hands.

"One, two, three!" Fiona and Josephine shouted as they all jumped into the water and had a special day.

No Pooping on the Dock! The Owl and the Looney, Whacky, Crazy and Naughty Ducks!

Written by: Kristine Ochu

Inspired by: Fiona and Josephine Mingus

Illustrated by: Kristine Ochu with gratitude for the guidance of Robin Marcus

Author can be contacted at: kristineochu@yahoo.com

Library of Congress Control Number: 2018901169

CreateSpace Independent Publishing Platform, North Charleston, SC

ISBN 10: 1983566802
ISBN 13: 978-1983566806

ABOUT THE AUTHOR AND INSPIRATION FOR THE STORY

Dear Readers,

I grew up on Lake Windigo, located outside of Hayward, Wisconsin. I was surrounded by nature that spurred my imagination to write magical stories. I was also a one-time senior amateur World Champion log roller! Now Herbert Rush, my husband and our golden retrievers love sharing summers on the lake with our expansive family.

One summer we had a group of ducks that kept pooping on our dock! We couldn't stop them and bought an owl statue to scare them off. My granddaughters, Fiona and Josephine loved to play with the owl but wanted to understand why he stayed on the dock. So I created a story about the owl coming alive to guard the dock and chase away the ducks. I had to tell the story every day!

Fall arrived and we headed back to Florida. I immediately got a call from my daughter pleading me to write the story down on paper. My grandchildren were begging her to tell the story at bedtime and wouldn't go to sleep without it. So that was the inspiration for my first published children's book, *No Pooping on the Dock! The Owl and the Looney, Whacky, Crazy and Naughty Ducks.*

I look forward to sharing more fun stories based on adventures with all my grandchildren including, Fiona, Josephine, Dean, Joshua, Thomas and Joseph, plus more grandchildren to come! Thank you to my beautiful daughters, Kelly Mingus and Jennifer Staysniak, and their husbands David and Christopher for blessing me with the greatest gift in the world---grandchildren!

I wish you peace, health, happiness and the pleasure of reading books!

Kristine Ochu

Made in the USA
Columbia, SC
16 February 2018